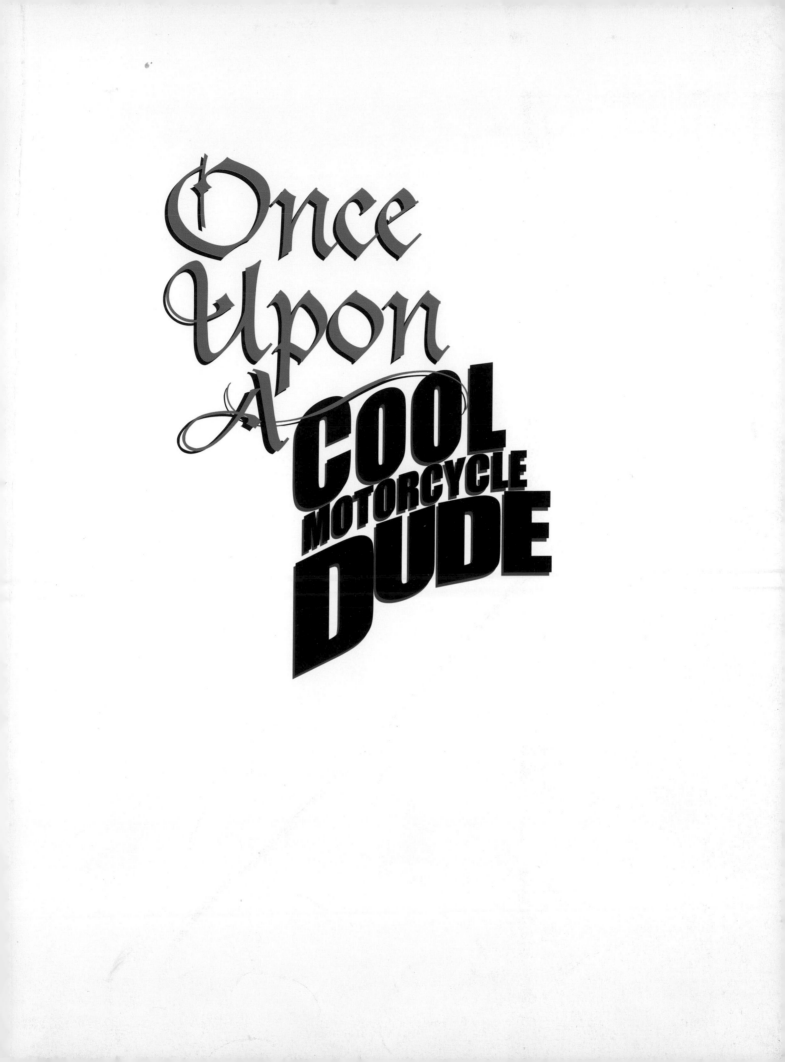

Once Upon A **COOL MOTORCYCLE DUDE**

For Scott Goto, Carol Heyer, and Cathy Evans.
—K. O.

For my godchildren, Chase Atkinson, Skylar Rae Atkinson,
Julia Ruiz, and Jessica Boudville. And, as always, to my
parents, William J. and Merlyn M. Heyer.
—C. H.

For all my bike-riding and non-bike-riding Dudes and
Dudettes, whom I call my friends.
—S. G.

First published in the United States of America in 2005 by
Walker Publishing Company, Inc.

Published simultaneously in Canada by
Fitzhenry and Whiteside, Markham, Ontario L3R 4T8

For information about permission to reproduce selections from this book, write
to Permissions, Walker & Company, 104 Fifth Avenue, New York, New York 10011

Library of Congress Cataloging-in-Publication Data
available upon request
ISBN 0-8027-8947-1 (hardcover)
ISBN 0-8027-8949-8 (reinforced)

Kevin O'Malley used pen and ink and digital color, Scott Goto used acrylic and oil
on paper, and Carol Heyer used acrylics to create the illustrations for this book.

Book design by Cathy Evans/Shoot the Moon

Visit Walker & Company's Web site at www.walkeryoungreaders.com

Printed in Hong Kong

2 4 6 8 10 9 7 5 3 1

Written and Illustrated by Kevin O'Malley

COOL MOTORCYCLE DUDE

Illustrated by Carol Heyer

Illustrated by Scott Goto

WALKER & COMPANY
NEW YORK

Once upon a time in a castle on a hill there lived a beautiful princess named Princess Tenderheart.

Every day Princess Tenderheart would play with her eight beautiful ponies. She named them Jasmie, Nimble, Sophie, and Polly. And Penny and Sunny and Monica . . .

Her favorite pony of all was called Buttercup.

One night a terrible thing happened. A giant came and stole away poor little Jasmie. All the other ponies cried and cried, but Princess Tenderheart cried hardest of all.

It was very sad.

The very next night the giant came and took Nimble and Sophie. Princess Tenderheart cried all day and refused to eat.

Oh please . . . get a grip, Princess!

Her father, the king, hired all the princes he could find to protect the ponies, but night after night another pony was stolen away.

The poor princess just sat in her room and turned straw into gold thread. She cried and cried and cried. When only Buttercup was left, Princess Tenderheart thought her heart would break.

Oh, who would protect Buttercup?

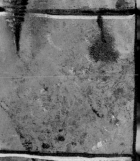

That's it . . . I can't take it anymore. I'll tell the story from here.

One day this really cool muscle dude rides up to the castle on his motorcycle. He says he'll guard the last pony if the king gives him all the gold thread that the princess makes. The king says okay, and the dude sits and waits for the giant.

As if . . .
He's not even cute or anything.

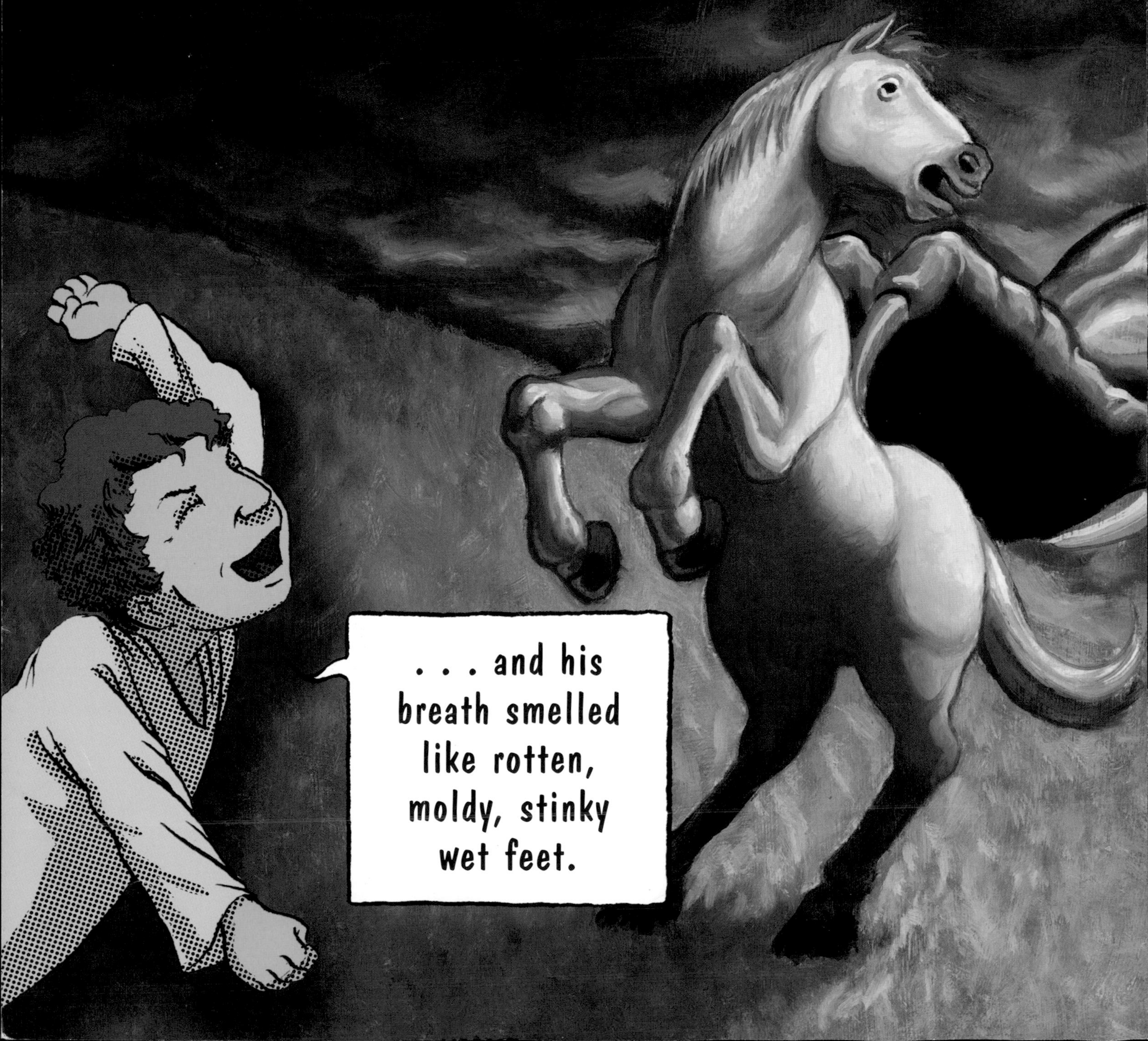
. . . and his breath smelled like rotten, moldy, stinky wet feet.

That's just gross!

He needs eight ponies to make a tasty pony stew and he only has seven. So that night he goes to steal the last horsey.

The muscle dude has this really big sword. The giant and the dude battled all over the place. The Earth was shaking and there was lightning and thunder and volcanoes were exploding.

It was HUGE!

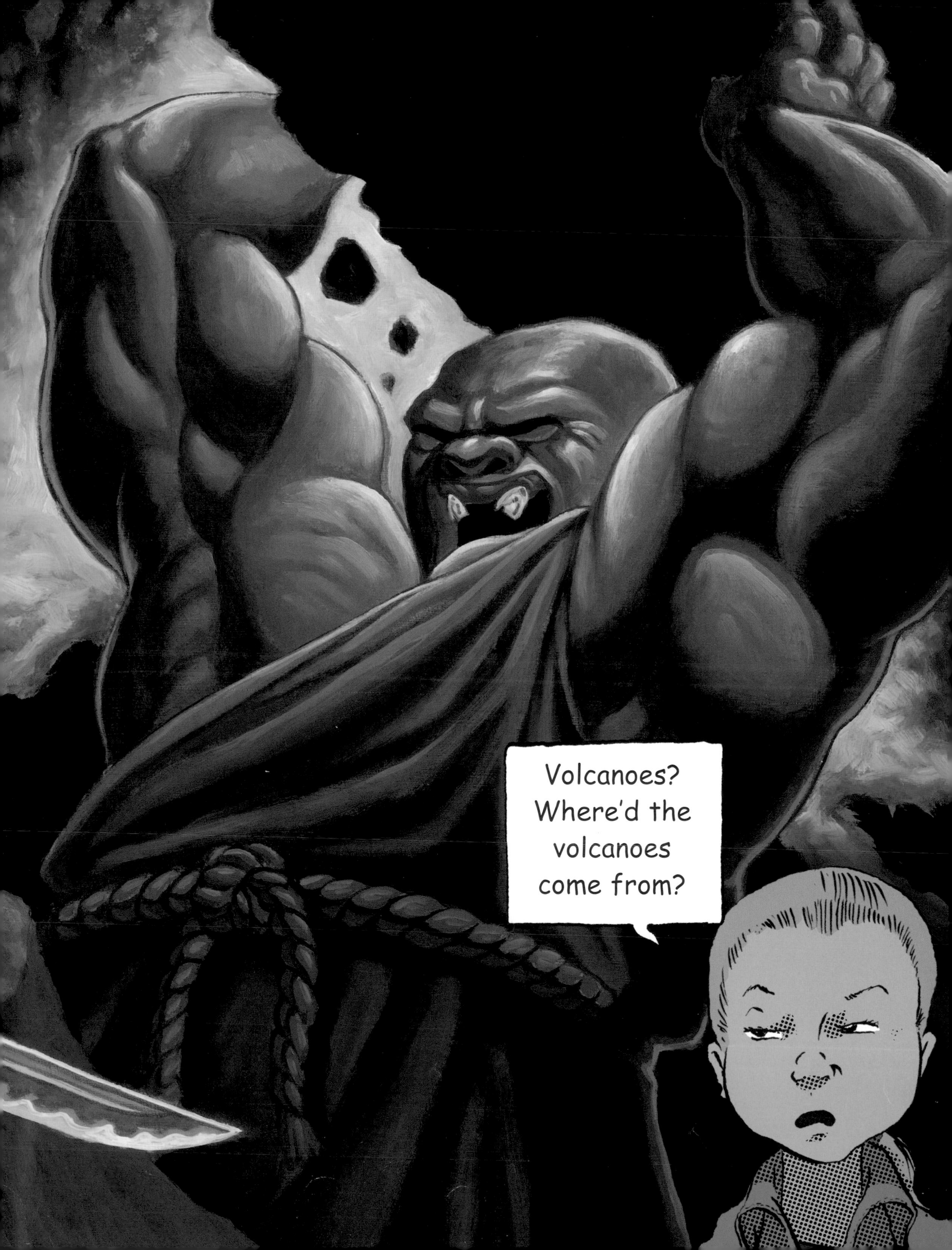
Volcanoes? Where'd the volcanoes come from?

Night after night the giant comes back, but the dude beats him. Night after night the princess makes gold thread and gives it to the dude. He gets really RICH . . .

Princess Tenderheart goes to the gym and pumps iron.
She becomes **Princess Warrior**.

VERY COOL!

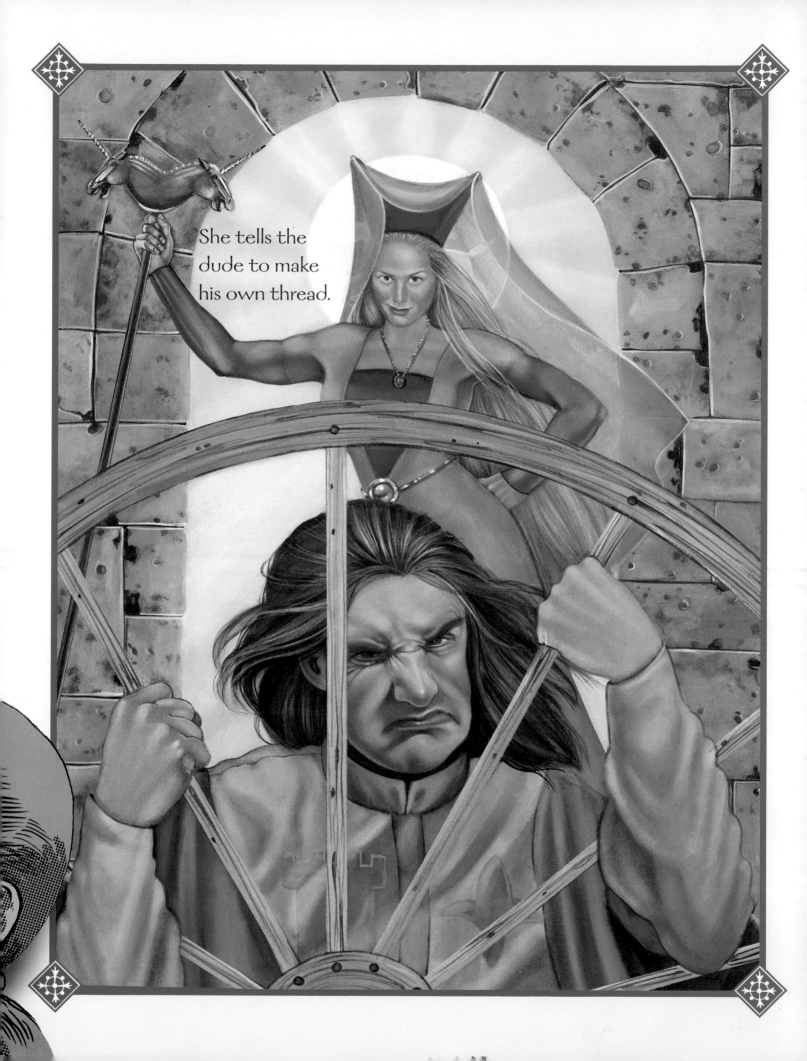

So that night the princess has
this huge and tremendous battle.
The giant runs back to his cave.

The
End.

The dude makes this really cool blanket out of the gold thread, and when he puts it over his head he turns INVISIBLE. Then he goes to rescue the ponies.

You can't see me!

The dude and the princess get into this big fight over who gets to free the ponies. *The giant hears voices and gets so scared he jumps off the cliff.*

The End.